Helping Hedgehog Home
Published by Graffeg in 2019
Copyright © Graffeg Limited 2019

Text and photographs copyright © Karin Celestine,
design and production Graffeg Limited.
This publication and content is protected by
copyright © 2019.

Karin Celestine is hereby identified as the author
of this work in accordance with section 77 of the
Copyrights, Designs and Patents Act 1988.

A CIP Catalogue record for this book is available
from the British Library.

ISBN 9781912213634

1 2 3 4 5 6 7 8 9

For more fun with the Tribe visit
www.celestineandthehare.com

Celestine and the Hare
Helping Hedgehog Home
by Karin Celestine

This book belongs to

GRAFFEG

Meet the Water Vole family

Bertram likes to sew. He is kind and helpful and sews for his family and other creatures. He uses old clothes left behind by people to make new things. He is happy with who he is and being a bit different to the other water voles.

Bert is Bertram's dad and likes to garden. He has an allotment and grows plants for his friends and all the creatures that live there. His favourite thing is to have a cup of tea and a biscuit and a snooze in his allotment shed.

Grandpa Burdock knows all the names of flowers and creatures and loves Bertram. He makes Bertram laugh by being silly and he thinks that while growing old is inevitable, growing up is optional. Grandpa also bakes the best cakes.

Granny Dandelion is very clever and can fix almost anything. She likes to use the rubbish that humans leave lying around to make useful things for the family. She gives Bertram extra cuddles while his mum is away exploring.

Beatrice is Bertram's mum. She is an explorer and inventor and made an airship from plastic bottles that had been thrown into the river. Beatrice is currently travelling up to the North Pole to help the polar bears.

Celestine and the Hare

Karin Celestine lives in a small house in Monmouth, Wales. In her garden there is a shed and in that shed is another world. The world of Celestine and the Hare.

It is a world where weasels are ruled by King Norty, pandas ride space hoppers and bears read stories to each other. It is a place that makes people smile and where kindness is the order of the day. All are welcome.

Karin taught children, about art, about chemistry, numbers, crafts and magic, but she was always drawn back to the Shed where she brings to life creatures of all kinds using only wool, observation and the power of imagination.

Karin and the creatures love stories and kindness, books and choklit and making things, and on Sundays they have Danish pastries, but not the apricot ones because they are frankly wrong.

Celestine, her great grandmother and namesake, watches over all in the shed and the hare sits with her; old wisdom helping the Tribe along their path in life.

Celestine and the Hare
Helping Hedgehog Home

For Tamsin and her Circus Mouse
who love and care for hedgehogs.

Also, with huge gratitude to John Ward,
Assistant Draftsman to Burdock Vole.

Granny Dandelion loves making things.
One day she went out to look for a tin can
to use in her latest invention.

Grandpa Burdock was settling down to
see if anyone new had moved into the
pond.

He was just about to say 'Hello!' to a water snail, when suddenly the sky went dark.

When he looked up, there was a hedgehog in a hot air balloon, about to crash into the pond!

Crash! Splash!

'Are you all right?' he shouted to the hedgehog, as he ran to help her.

'Oh, erm, sorry, yes, sorry, I think so, thank you,' said the hedgehog. 'I... I... I'm so so sorry to frighten you like that,' she spluttered, brushing watercress from her prickles.

Grandpa helped her out on to dry land and then quietly waited a moment, despite having a million things he wanted to ask her.

Hedgehogs need a moment to gather their skirts and smooth their prickles before answering lots of questions.

'What on earth happened?' he asked, when she had recovered a little and he couldn't hold in his excitement any longer.

'While I was out looking for dinner,
they built a new fence and my gap to get
into the garden has gone. I love my little
leafy log pile.

'I can't get home.

'I built this balloon from rubbish I
collected in the hedgerows to try and
fly back. But I'm too prickly and
I popped it and crashed.'

'Well now,' said Grandpa. 'First of all, let's have a nice cup of tea and then we will plan how to fly you back home. My wife, Dandelion, will be home soon and she's amazing at building things. We'll have a think what to do and she'll sort it out when she gets back.'

'Thank you,' sniffed the hedgehog.

Bertram brought out a lovely cup of tea and Grandpa's freshly-baked bramble biscuits and they sat quietly for a while.

While the hedgehog drank her tea, Grandpa, who couldn't wait any longer, got out his paper and pencils and started drawing ideas to help her home. As he drew, he became more and more excited.

fuse

Soup-plate blast protector

GRANDPA BURDOCK'S
COAL-SCUTTLE CANNON

gunpowder
goes here

'Oh! Oh! I know!' shouted Grandpa.
'Dandelion's got an old coal scuttle in
her workshop. We could turn it into a
cannon and blast you over!'

Hedgehog gulped and sipped her tea
nervously.

'I... erm... I'm not sure how safe that is...'

soup-plate blast protector

GRANDPA BURDOCK'S
COAL-SCUTTLE CANNON

gunpowder goes here

3. landing

1. blast off

2. separation

Rocket
fuel goes
here

CACHE

pull
chain
to blast off

grip
handles

hedgehog gasbeeze

gramophone
horn
afterburner

parachute   parakeet

GRANDPA BURDOCK'S
ROCKET THUNDERBOX
(with gramophone horn
after burner)

Labels in diagram:
1. Blast off
2. separation
3. landing
rocket fuel goes here
hedgehog goes here
pull chain to blast off
grip handles
parachute
parakeet
gramophone horn afterburner
ACME
GRANDPA BURDOCK'S
ROCKET THUNDERBOX
(with gramophone horn afterburner)

'Hmm,' said
Grandpa. 'Handles
to hold on to,
that's what we
need. Handles!'
He drew again.

'Look! We could make a thunderbox and
flush you over!' he exclaimed, flinging yet
more drawings her way.

'Oh gosh, you are inventive. Erm, perhaps
something a little less explosive?' she
suggested gently.

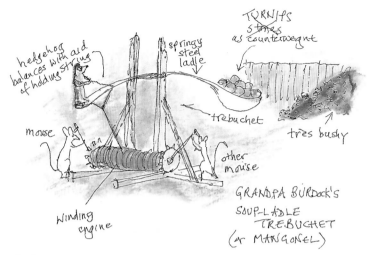

hedgehog balances with aid of holding string

springy steel ladle

TURNIPS stones as counterweight

mouse

trebuchet

other mouse

très bushy

GRANDPA BURDOCK'S
SOUP-LADLE
TREBUCHET
(or MANGONEL)

winding engine

'Oh, right-ho! Let's see...

'I know! We can make a catapult out of
a soup ladle! A hedgehog trebuchet!
Or should that be a hedgehogapult?'
He giggled as he showed her the drawing.
'You'll like this one! No explosions!'

Hedgehog looked worried and had another
sip of her tea, not daring to say anything.

last projector

how it works

full tension   2. cable cut   **3.** hedgehog flies through the air

hedgehog balances with aid of holding string

springy steel ladle

mouse

trebu

winding engine

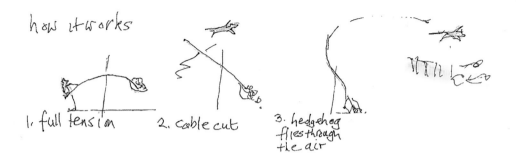

how it works

1. full tension   2. cable cut   3. hedgehog flies through the air

Grandpa excitedly drew lots of plans for the trebuchet.

Hedgehog sat silently, getting more worried.

Just as Hedgehog was thinking it might be better just to find a new home, Granny Dandelion appeared.

'I found my tin can, Burdock!' she called, 'Any biscuits left?'

'Oh, hello, how lovely to meet you!' she said, spying the hedgehog nervously looking at the drawings.

Grandpa explained about Hedgehog's plight. Granny listened carefully and smiled.

'Oh don't you worry, my dear, we will soon have you home.'

Hedgehog nodded her thanks, but inside she was worrying about what terrible contraption Granny might be about to build.

Granny smiled and disappeared straight off to her workshop.

They heard a lot of sawing and hammering.

Bertram gave Hedgehog his teddy to cuddle while they waited.

After a long wait, Granny Dandelion came back, calling, 'Ready!'

Grandpa jumped up, shouting, 'Kaboom!' and 'Fling!'

Hedgehog followed them very, very slowly, not daring to look.

'Here! I've made you a door in the fence,' said Granny. 'Now you can come and go whenever you like.'

'Oh! Oh! Thank you!' gasped Hedgehog. She started to cry with relief and happiness.

Granny gave her a cuddle and said, 'Please come and visit us. I'll ask Grandpa to make us a cake. He's good at that and they don't usually explode.'

'Thank you,' said Hedgehog. 'Thank you. I'd love that very much. Thank you for looking after me so kindly, both of you.'

And then she opened the door and scurried off home.

The next day, Granny and Grandpa found a surprise by the door.

Thank you, Grandpa Burdock.

Thank you, Granny Dandelion.

Make your own papier-mâché hot air balloon

You will need:

- Some torn up newspaper or scrap paper
- PVA glue mixed with water
- A yoghurt or plant pot
- A balloon
- String

1. Blow up the balloon to the size and shape you would like your hot air balloon to be. If you are bigger than a hedgehog, it can be helpful to put the balloon on a bowl so you can reach all the sides.

2. Cover the balloon in pieces of torn up newspaper dipped in the glue mixture. Make sure the bits of paper overlap and cover the whole balloon except for the very bottom. Do 2-3 layers and then leave it to dry.

3. When dry, pop the balloon with a pin and make a *phhhhffft* noise (or sometimes a bang!). Pull the balloon out and put in the bin. Cut the edges to make a neat hole at the bottom. You can either paint it or cover it with nice paper. You can also decorate it with ribbon, pretty paper or stickers, like the mice have done on the next page.

4. Find something to make a basket; you can have a look in the recycling bin for a suitable container, such as an old yoghurt pot. You can paint the container or cover it with paper or stickers too.

5. Tie the string around the basket and loop it over the top of the balloon, or carefully poke holes in the basket

and balloon to thread it through and tie knots to hold in place.

6. You can hang the balloon up from your ceiling by a thread or wire on the top and maybe put one of your teddies in it for a fly around.

Send your pictures of your balloon to Graffeg, email croeso@graffeg.com.

Hedgehog was lucky to have Dandelion and Burdock to help her. Hedgehogs in your garden might not be so lucky, so Grandpa asked his friends Kyra and Sophie, the girls from Hedgehog Friendly Town, to tell us what we can do to help hedgehogs in our gardens.

Interesting facts about hedgehogs

1. Hedgehogs are really good swimmers.

2. Hedgehogs are nocturnal, so should be seen only at night.

3. Hedgehogs can detect an earthworm or beetle under 7.5cm of soil.

4. Hedgehogs have an amazing sense of smell but poor eyesight.

5. Hedgehogs hibernate over the winter, dropping their heart rate and body temperature so they can sleep for many months.

Ways you can help hedgehogs

1. Make a hedgehog pathway into one or more of your garden boundaries. It only needs to be 13 x 13cm.

2. Make a feeding station specially for hedgehogs.

3. Put a ramp or steps in your pond to help them climb out.

4. Don't use slug pellets. They poison hedgehogs.

5. Check bonfires before lighting.

You can find out lots more about how to help hedgehogs, such as how to build a feeding station, on their website: www.hedgehogfriendlytown.co.uk.